CHATO AND THE PARTY ANIMALS

by GARY SOTO
ILLUSTRATED by SUSAN GUEVARA

G.P. Putnam's Sons
NEW YORK

LET'S PARTY!

Library of Congress Cataloging-in-Publication Data Soto, Gary. Chato and the party animals / by Gary Soto; illustrated by Susan Guevara. p. cm.
Summary: Chato decides to throw a "pachanga" for his friend Novio Boy, who has never had a birthday party. [1. Cats—Fiction. 2. Parties—Fiction. 3. Birthdays—Fiction. 4. Los Angeles (Calif.)—Fiction.] I. Guevara, Susan, ill. II. Title. PZ7.S7242 Cj 2000 [E]—dc21 96-037501
ISBN 0-399-23159-5   10 9 8 7 6 5 4 3 2 1   FIRST IMPRESSION

GLOSSARY

carnal	brother
comida	meal
el barrio	the neighborhood
grito	loud yell
Las Mañanitas	traditional birthday song
lo mejor	the best
mami	mommy
mercado	market
mi familia	my family
muy	very
pachanga	festive party
piñata	papier-mâché container filled with candy
pobrecito	poor little thing
¿Por qué?	Why?
pues	well
¡Qué tonto!	How dumb!
refritos	refried beans
¡Simón!	Of course!
suavecito	handsome guy
vatos	guys, dudes

To Mary Rose Ortega and the teachers of First Street Elementary. — G.S.

For the Border Kids. — S.G.

A party animal since he was a kitten, Chato was catnip-crazy to be at Chorizo's birthday party. The mice next door had invited the whole neighborhood to celebrate the dog's birthday. The party-goers played shake-paws, juggle-the-mice, and toss-the-cat-in-the-blanket.

Hay Mas Tiempo Que Vida

¡Feliz Cumpleaños, CHORIZO!

Mami mouse
served dog biscuits as
appetizers. To be polite, Chato
threw a couple in his mouth.
"What do you think?" Chato
whispered to Novio Boy.
"These are breaking
my teeth," Novio Boy
mumbled back.
Chato swallowed his
dog biscuits and
sniffed the air.
"Who's cutting the
cheese?" he asked,
delighted by the smell.
"Try some,"
Papi mouse said.
Chato stuffed his
furry face, but his
friend Novio Boy
hung his head and
said, "No, thanks.
I don't feel hungry."
His eyelashes were
shining with tears.

"What's wrong?"
Chato asked his friend.
Novio Boy didn't answer.

"Come on, cat," Chato begged.
"I'm your best friend."

"Birthday parties always
do this to me," Novio Boy said.

"*¿Por qué?* Why, dude?" asked Chato.

"I'm from the pound," Novio Boy
purred sadly. "I don't know when I was
born. I never knew my *mami*. I never
even had a birthday party, or nothing."

Chato wrapped his tail around
the shoulders of his friend.

"It doesn't matter," Novio Boy
sighed. "Who cares about things like that?
Stupid balloons and games and presents
and all the milk you can drink."

But Chato could see that Novio Boy
did care. His best friend went home,
dragging his tail.

"Pobrecito. Everybody needs a birthday party,"
Chato said to himself when he got home.
"I'm going to give my *carnal* a party!"

Chato telephoned Blanca's Bakery. He ordered
a large cake with mouse-colored frosting.

"And put a couple of canaries on top," Chato added.

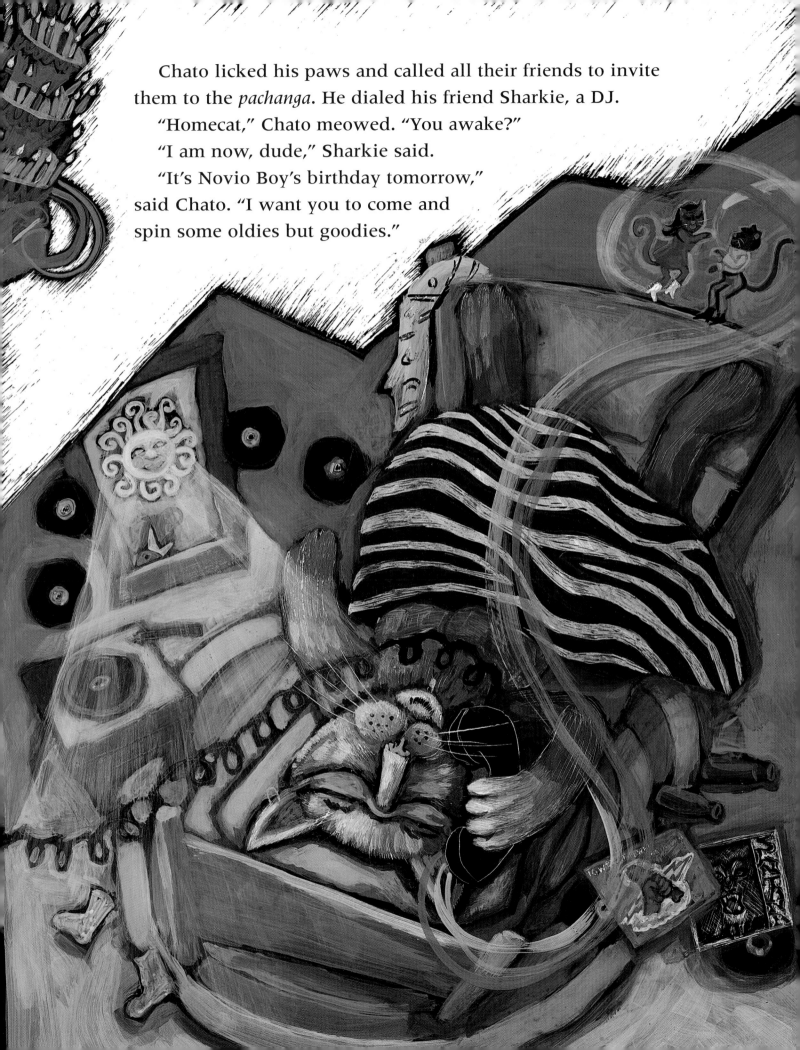

Chato licked his paws and called all their friends to invite them to the *pachanga*. He dialed his friend Sharkie, a DJ.

"Homecat," Chato meowed. "You awake?"

"I am now, dude," Sharkie said.

"It's Novio Boy's birthday tomorrow," said Chato. "I want you to come and spin some oldies but goodies."

The next morning, Chato
made a *piñata* out of newspaper
and an empty cat food box.
He picked up the cake and party
favors. He bought flea combs,
collars with shiny bells,
wind-up mice, and half-priced
yarn that was already a mess
of tangles.

Then he slinked over to
the *mercado*. He bought cream
and cat crunchies, cheese
and dog biscuits, and extra
kitty litter just in case.

Back home, Chato started
a pot of beans boiling for *refritos*.
He made guacamole and fresh
salsa. He pressed pawprints
into tortillas, his specialty.

He filled water balloons
and dragged the sofa
onto the patio for
everyone to jump on.
He sprinkled catnip
and hid dog bones
in the flowerbed.
"Don't you think of
messing with me,
homedog,"
Chato joked in
the face of an
inflatable dog.

The twins, Mas and Menos, were the first to arrive, followed
by Flirty, Samba, Pelon, and Pelon's three-month-old son, Peloncito.
Chorizo cruised onto the patio with the family of mice on his back.
"Where's the birthday cat?" Chorizo asked.

Chato's face went blank.

"Oh, no! *¡Qué tonto!* I think I forgot to invite him!"

"You forgot to tell Novio Boy?" Chorizo asked.

Chato nodded his head.

"Pues, let's go round up that birthday cat," Chorizo suggested.

They barked, meowed, and squeaked through the neighborhood. More cats and dogs and at least three mice joined them. Novio Boy was nowhere to be found. He was not in the sycamore tree, on top of Señora Ramirez's garage roof, or sleeping on a warm car fender— all the places where he liked to kick back. "Maybe he's hurt," Chato worried.

They checked the gutters to see if he was run over, flat as a tortilla.

"He's gone," Chato moaned. "My *carnal* has been kidnapped."

"Maybe our homecat's just lost," Sharkie said.

"Kidnapped! Lost!" Mas and Menos cried, shivering from their two worst fears.

Back at Chato's place the party animals sat on the patio. None of them touched the cake or water balloons or the blow-up German shepherd.

"He was such a *sauvecito*," Sharkie said.

"*Ló mejor*. The best," Chato said, choking on his tears.

"I miss him," Samba sighed.

"I remember when we used to hang in the trees, pretending we were birds," Chato continued. "It was so much fun."

"And I remember he was always a sharp dresser," Sharkie said. "And *muy* kind."

"Courageous!" Pelon said. "He always backed me up in fights."

"Respectful," Papi mouse recalled. "He made me feel like a giant."

"And his eyes," Flirty purred. "They were so gorgeous."

"Too bad this *vato* is gone," Novio Boy butted in.
"He sounds like someone I'd like to hang with."
Every cat, dog, and mouse turned to look at him.
"Novio Boy!" Chato screamed.
"You're not kidnapped? You're not dead?"

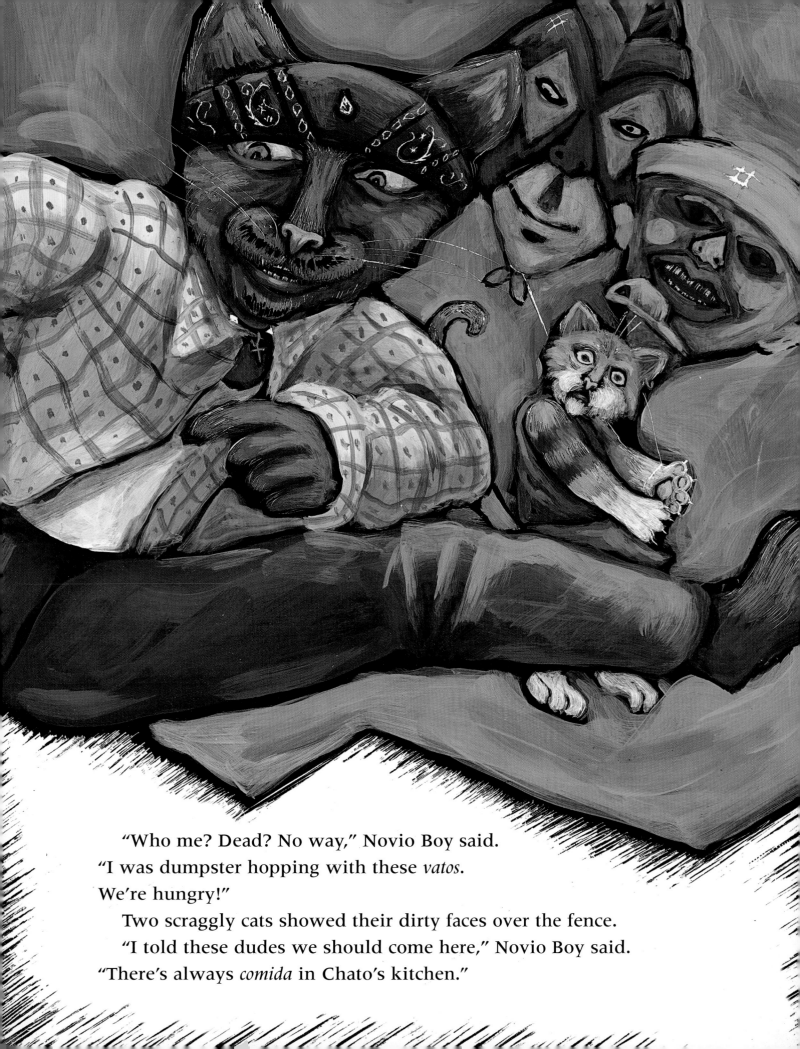

"Who me? Dead? No way," Novio Boy said.
"I was dumpster hopping with these *vatos*.
We're hungry!"
    Two scraggly cats showed their dirty faces over the fence.
    "I told these dudes we should come here," Novio Boy said.
"There's always *comida* in Chato's kitchen."

Chato sprang up and gave
the signal for the *grito*.
"SURPRISE!"
everyone yelled.
"Surprise?" asked
Novio Boy.
"Yeah, it's your
birthday!" Chato said.
"No."
"*¡Simón!*" Chato cried.
"You must have been born
on the first day of summer.
That's why you like
to play so much, *carnal*!"
Novio Boy grinned a
full set of teeth.
"OK, you party animals,"
Sharkie crowed.
"Let's dance!"

The animals ate and partied hearty. They tossed water balloons at each other, purposely missing because they knew wet fur was no fun. Then Chorizo taught them "Going to the Vet," where you had to scream your head off.

"Piñata time!" Chato meowed loudly. All of them got a chance, but it was Novio Boy who, on his third big-league swing, broke open the catfish piñata.

After they sang
"Las Mañanitas,"
Novio Boy cut the cake
and licked the
frosting from the
canaries' feet.
He opened
his presents.
    "This is the
best birthday
party I've
ever been
to," Novio
Boy said.
    "Better than
the dumpsters?"
Chato asked.
    "*¡Simón!*
You guys are *mi familia*,"
Novio Boy said.
    "You're the best."

The *pachanga* lasted until the sun went down, the moon came up, and the neighbors started throwing shoes at them to stop the racket. Novio Boy stayed overnight, sleeping on a new cat cushion, his present from Chato, the coolest *carnal* in all of *el barrio*.